SLOW
Lie
detector

To Kate Sipples,
a great
fellow writer

SLOW
Lie
detector

Les plesko

Equator Books
Venice

Published by Equator Books
1103 Abbot Kinney Blvd
Venice, CA 90291

Published in the United States of America
Printed in Canada

First Printing

ISBN: 978-0-9669188-2-3

Library of Congress Catalog Number: 2009921362

Visit the Equator Books website at:
www.equatorbooks.com

For
Eireene Nealand

running

How do you make a film? Always bring your camera along. Hold the camera still. Put a person, a sermon in there; make sure there's enough light.

A woman who stood by the roadside: you'd stop. She didn't bother to stick out her thumb, blue smoke disappeared from a van or a truck in a water mirage. He filmed her holding her broken shoe strap, her hair made its own whimsical breeze as she got in the used-to-be-red Maverick.

No bag, she said as if she represented unabashed freedom itself. Her voice had that camera to subject distance that he already liked. She picked loose M&M's from the seat and from under herself and ate them. She showed him her chocolaty teeth, the candy like tiny enamel eggshells in her mouth.

Hold the wheel, he said while he filmed out the window, his foot on the gas.

Her blue skirt rode up, Air Force jets shivered the car, he filmed that, the road into town like a ribbon that might have been snapped, then he put down his camera to take the wheel back.

He'd already filmed all the gray desert scrub he could stand, pupfish in winter lakebeds, the silence between if and when a car passed. His bare-ankled shins, his wingtips, his pant legs. The weight of light. The body's loneliness.

He was thinking that she was exactly as tall as he was. It wasn't strange not to talk: except in the store to say *thanks*, he hadn't spoken for a month.

Sometimes it seemed like space aliens came, they planted a chip in his brain that only resembled a past.

There used to be the kind of quiet only one person can have. Then she'd got in his car.

Why make a movie? Because he can? Has?

What he wants are not subjects of thought but just things as they are: cinderblock, tinderbox. It was mystery enough that everything was as it was.

Razorblades, tape, with these he cut film among dust and sand flies, his light box a neon aquarium lamp, his black suit gone gray from sunlight. Only spring and already he had just the memory of rain, the motel's burnt stucco washed pink, the rooms holding their line in the sand.

What he'd filmed so far: cactus wrens among brittlebush. Flora and fauna, the two seasons—cold and hot. Winn shielding her eyes in the car between Argus and Darwin, the no water 20 miles sign.

Winn at the small metal desk that's too cramped for her legs, on the edge of his bed in the room third from left at the Notice of Pending Eviction motel.

Proximity bothered him.

She didn't mind that he watched as she washed her dress in the sink in her white underwear, not so white.

Immodest by necessity, she turned from his lens, her blue dress hung darker blue wet.

Winsome, Winnifred, Guenevir, she hadn't said what her name stood for yet. Her teeth were like baby teeth only large but translucent like that.

He said, I don't know what this movie's about but you're going to be in it because everything gets into it.

The Bolex was propped on the chair, she said everything gets into everything, Max. Like she didn't bring clothes so now she wore his. He had half: half his toothbrush, she drank from his glass.

It had been a while since a woman had spoken his name, even privately to herself, he'd have guessed.

Don't think just film.

She was pale she was tall she'd burn quick in the sun.

Here's Winn getting out of the car, *no don't wave* but too late.

They stood in a dry riverbed, he said you can't step in the same river twice. Even once, she said. That old hoary koan: if a tree falls and no one's around . . .

You could see rain on the Amargosa Range but it never touched ground, then a flash flood had washed the road, flushed out the woodrat middens. He filmed dark standing pools and Winn barefoot in them. China Lake's jets' streaked contrails reflected in puddles outside the Eviction motel.

With Winn around, he felt his clothes and his body in them.

At night, bare-chested, he cut film. Mostly she stayed two doors down while the light in his room was like underwatery television. He'd been splicing old footage, what-was-he-thinking, can't-tell-what-you're-looking-at stuff. The rain didn't stop. She knocked on his door: who can sleep through all this?

The weather or him two doors down.

Winn on the edge of his bed, the kind motels have with small wheels and a wafer mattress. They played crazy eights on the floor among curled strips of film. He gambled away M&M's while his radio played static from lightning on Panamint Hill. They played for his clothes and her dress and he put it on because who could see them?

She looked up from his bed. Wasn't it obvious what she meant?

Do you want to, even? she said, because once we start we won't stop. She laughed: that old joke: *don't! stop!*

Or don't even begin, because there's a lot they didn't know about each other yet. As if that ever made a difference.

She put on her shoes because things cut your feet when you walked to your room in the dark—Winn's wide mouth, her long hands—in his film he'd been filming cautious depictions of small happiness.

This straight-standing habit she had in his doorway at night in a towel and a towel on her head: her shoulders a bar, you could balance teacups on them. He guessed he was twenty years older than her, he thought he had twenty years left. He told her for six years he'd been celibate but he didn't mind, much.

She said, expectation is good for your film, isn't it? Except he had tried to quit that. He'd read a book about Zen, a Zen joke if you thought about it: who can take a single step with his head?

She wore that talcum powder he liked that smelled like a pleasant affront: she smelled like cold Nivea cream. She had her mysteries, like how did she get to the store and what did she use to buy things; in Darwin who sold Nivea cream?

Sometimes he thought he should explain himself but she said, I already know: you feel this you feel that.

He smiled because he liked to be talked about by a girl barely dressed; the best understanding he had of himself was always secondhand.

I bet you fall for women with problems and you try to help them, Winn said.

He'd filmed that smiling helplessness, he thought they'd been complicated. He kept on confusing interesting traits with stubborn weaknesses.

I bet you think love is compassion, Winn said.

He opened his palms. He used to play records at night to make feelings come or to get rid of them. He'd always imagined the worst to make himself ready for it but Winn stood in the cool evening dew, she shook her wet hair loose for him, she looked cool as a green succulent.

Now he had what to film: Winn in the bed of a two-hundred-century lake with her feet in the Pleistocene. She played his old Leonard Cohen cassette with that towel wrapped over her breasts like the picture that old album had.

He kept shining the camera light in her eyes. Do you want me to stop?

Don't stop. Do your job.

Here's the concrete cistern where they swam, three-legged tadpoles in there, blind triple-eyed single-finned fish. Winn wore a pink bathing cap while overhead, jets shined their bright spacecraft lights, tipped their fins.

She kept scraping her legs, from his room back to hers, on the cruel cactuses. He felt too old for this not sleeping with Winn; old enough though to keep his hands on the Bolex.

Ophir Mine, Ballarat, each time they got in his car, the whole desert got in with them. She said, I used to ride the Greyhound, I made some distance. Those fat men on the bus: cowboys, *bus*boys. The wind took her laugh about it.

If he got her to drive he could film with both hands the wild dogs running after his car. Or what if she drove away in the Maverick that used to be red? But that risk was a test.

She drove right off the road, she drove into a cactus, a rock. She drove with her arm out the window, she sang la la la la la la, she said look Max no hands.

He said Jesus quit fooling around; the car wobbled, pulled hard to the left.

She said hey I made you mad! You should practice your Zen.

They sat in the car to try it while the hot engine ticked. He laughed, he said, so when does not thinking begin?

One day there were flowers, then *bang*, summer fell like a bright guillotine.

He read his massive tomes, Winn sprawled in his chair reading *Tristes Tropiques*. They took shallow baths in the galvanized tub when the air broke a hundred degrees carelessly like you break a light sweat climbing stairs, if there had been stairs.

These gigantical books, Winn said. These doorstops. These volumes you prop your camera on.

What the world needs is more shoes, not my movie, he said. The heat let you say anything.

Winn made strawberry jam sandwiches. When the wind got too loud she slept beside him.

In your dreams, who's that *Werner?* she said.

My father who left me at the orphanage, Maximilian said. He didn't want to go down memory lane, a long but narrow street.

I guess you don't miss the past much, Winn said.

He'd ridden with Werner to Saint Boniface while sheet music fluttered around in the car, Werner tapping some queer melody on the seat between them.

Later he drove with the Glenlivet tucked in his legs while rain slicked the pavement.

Nostalgia's just longing for romance, he said.

That's you, Max, that's what you do, Winn said. He thought she was laughing, but nicely, at him.

Anyway Werner's dead Maximilian said like a fact about it.

Winn picked strawberry seeds from her teeth, she said yeah that's what happens to everyone, man.

"Man," he liked that; the sun set like an accordion.

She moved closer to him in her loose white tee shirt with red jam on her breath. She put a sandwich in her mouth and then his, she said, here, have a sweet Madeleine.

Winn scraped calluses from her heels, her feet cut from barefootedness and filmstrips. She sat on his bed fooling with bandages.

He watched her comb out her hair. Already she was a future picture in his brain, like some cool-eyed insurance for remembering, later on. This wasn't how he'd have wanted to be if he could choose how he was.

A taxi arrived with her things.

Darwin's so small anyone's findable here, anybody can come to Darwin.

Winn laid out her clothes on his bed, she sprayed them with freshener and put them inside plastic bags. She said, they make these airtight.

Still, he said, sand'll get into them.

Sand blew into the room while Winn modeled her white dress.

That taxi, he said, because what about it bothered him?

Winn smiled warily. She told him her dream: we swam nude then we ate M&M's.

A whole month had passed so whatever happened between them would have calculation in it.

These tiny buttons! Winn made her fingers look helpless on the dress.

He thought when it happened he'd let her begin because he'd never been sober for this, but then they'd already started, they had no clothes on in daylight on the small bed.

She said, this isn't because of the dream.

Okay, he said. It was that cab, he thought, but so what.

She looked fuller naked—narrowings, widenesses. His hands had forgot all the small and large things about womanliness. He'd forgot he missed them.

She said wait, here, okay? They helped each other past the where-do-we-put-our-knees parts.

It was like the difference between a roadmap and then you stop the car and get out and the road's shivering in the heat.

Now you'll be gooky about me, Winn said, kind of suddenly sad. They were eating her Sno Balls and his M&M's from a plate on the floor between then.

So, listen, Winn said. About that.

That taxicab that keeps driving by. He'd filmed it. A taxi with out of state plates that got lost getting off the turnpike.

He'd already filmed Winn with only the plate in her lap, licking her fingers to tamp up the coconut sprinkles she placed on his tongue.

Listen, I'm married, she said with pink coconut on her lips.

Ah, he said. But at least he had got her on film. He said, it's the guy driving that cab.

She nodded. My husband, she said in the dark. They had let it get dark.

Well, she hadn't promised anything.

He'd been with women with husbands before. Everything would be guilty and significant, though that could be all right. He wouldn't be responsible if Winn was somebody's wife.

She wiped her sticky hands on his knees. He's a sailor from Jersey she said as if that explained everything.

They breathed quietly for a while, listening for car sounds, then she crawled on her hands and knees toward the bed like she'd hide from sweeping headlights, laughing between her fingers on her mouth.

So, I missed him, Winn said. I'm thirty-eight, Max, I was seventeen then.

Hadn't this happened before—him lying in bed with a woman, talking about someone else. But he had gestures of Winn he still wanted to film: how she peed with the bathroom door wide. He wanted that moment to last when she hadn't yet come back to bed but she would, in a minute.

She found him by feel in the dark. I might have planned this but that doesn't mean we can't like it, she said.

running toward

By now he doubted that dreaming was wishing for pleasure or sex. It's not pleasure we wish for but death.

Thinking like this always cheered Maximilian up.

Sometimes, he told Winn, I want to be cold and alone and inebriated.

The cold part will be difficult here, Max, she said.

The cab ticked though it wouldn't cool, here.

He watched the wind blow her hair beside him, and Richard in his sailor cap: how could anyone be so blonde, even his long eyelashes. Dick Legg washing the cab, splashing Winn with the rag like a real husband.

He took off his shirt so Maximilian could film his nuclear accident scars.

There was a meltdown in the core of a sub, Richard said, though you wouldn't have read about it.

Hard to look at, but Maximilian had the Bolex. He could stand a lot looking through that: the sailor returned but not from the sea and Winn so happy to see him.

They rode in the cab because hot wind blew on them at least. Winn must have felt pretty smart, she'd

21

got these two guys on each side. On the one hand, the other, what simply happened and what must, and then there was luck.

Richard climbed in the back, he said you drive, Max, like being seen tired him out. When his tee shirt rode up you could make out soft circles like coins. The tattoo that said Winn.

Winn said, he never lets anyone drive. He soaked up like a million rems, she said, like Dick wasn't right there with them. As if he was on the ocean. Under it.

Maximilian wondered if he was supposed to feel pity or what. He wanted to film what that was but how could he, he was part of it. Maybe Dick would drop dead. Bad thoughts were all right, only what you did counted and not what you thought, how you felt.

Anyway he liked Richard and Winn, they looked good through his lens. Anyhow, he had rules about how to live, his sober discipline.

Winn said, I'm too old for sailors in undershirts, Max, even if he's my husband. But he didn't think she meant it.

In the shade of a shade like Odysseus' sail, they drifted. Who'd have believed she was even still here, though no one was keeping her. Right? Did she want to be kept?

Summer! Jesus! Winn said. Hot wind blew from all directions. Maximilian thought it was money she worried about: not much left from the grant for his film he kept in the canister under the bed. The thin paper faith that makes fate.

Marx pawned his clothes and his family's clothes for the rent, Richard said.

So how did he get home? Winn said, or then get out of bed?

They were *in* bed, Winn pushed his shoulder on the left and Maximilian's on the other side. Or maybe Marx didn't get out of bed, or want to, Winn said.

They lay very narrowly, the blue sheet for keeping the flies off pulled up over them. I don't care that we're poor, do I, guys? Winn said.

Well, money, Dick said, flicked his wrist, but he kept his cab fares in a bank like a normal person.

Winn said, in France they don't talk about it.

23

Well, *this* is French-like, Dick said; he meant lying together, the blue light the sheet made on them.

Unlike France, though, Winn said, we're still dressed.

Maximilian watched her to see what he should think about this. M&M's in the bed, and salty corn chips.

Life and no escape, Maximilian said, though he meant it in a happy way: he'd trained himself for aloneness.

Winn blurped in the crook of Dick's arm and then his but how was this moving his movie along, for instance? Only funny and stupid and sad, a French film where no one has money, or works, and the rest, so he got up and got the Bolex. He was working on it.

What kind of a man had she liked? Let's say a sailor, tall and thin. Peripatetic: she'd looked it up.

She used to think all she needed was a hundred dollar bill she could hide in her shoe. A place to wash her underpants. She'd been running away from no one. He'd been fixing his truck in the street. Four-thirty a.m., he said, hand me that wrench. A 3/16-torque wrench, she guessed.

He hadn't looked up though he must have smelled her perfume, methedrine, and her cigarette smoke. Alcohol.

He'd be off to Guam in a week. *Will you wait?*

That's what sailors' babes do, she said, isn't it?

Dick rode them around Bywater Road looking for a carwash. Sailors' *wives* wait, he said.

She thought she could stand a hundred summers by the sea by a port where battleships berthed.

Rhode Island in spring where she watched for Dick's ship to come in. Washed her pink uniform in the sink, hung it from the ledge. Low-flying rooftops: her view, and telephone lines, and beyond them, though she couldn't see it, the sea. April showers, a rain and sea smell. A salty greenness. The pavement wet on Calendar Place two blocks from Farewell and she's only a little worried: what might Dick bring back from those ports-o-call girls?

Then you get a telegram.

Richard had been in the hold when the meltdown happened. He'd sloshed in knee-deep radium.

If you're going to suffer, don't linger, she'd said though he couldn't hear her behind leaded glass.

So what am I supposed to sit around wiping your bum?

And worse! Richard said. Blue wounds, miles of gauze.

They'd been married a month.

When light rose outside, she licked a Kleenex, wiped the sweat from Richard's forehead.

She'd brought over her little cassette with only Merle Haggard on it. She said, when I drink I'm this Merle Haggard nut.

Sure, who isn't? Maximilian said. There was something about a drunk woman he liked.

All afternoon she'd been swilling Kamchatka and now it was dusk. She said, did you drink because you felt bad or did drinking become the badness?

I was just killing time till it ended, he said.

Winn said, not with me now though, right? She kissed him on the mouth, she said what are we kissing about?

He wanted her long undressed whiteness on him; the purity of the drunken event, he'd missed that.

She said, I think I'm not what you like. I bet your fun was sad girls you loved when you loved to be sad.

He liked her drunk intuition about what he'd loved. That's us, doll, he said. He missed calling girls that.

Doll, she said, that's nice, Max. She leaned against him, she said Richard's in Trona buying car parts. She looked toward the bed without ambivalence, she tried pulling her dress past her head without putting the bottle aside. It's some kind of cruel trick, she said, tangled up. Drunks were so obvious, though she wasn't as drunk as she might have wanted to seem, Maximilian thought.

She watched him significantly from the bed. Dick and me never bought rings, she told him, because we had our trust. She shrugged, she turned Merle Haggard off. Never mind, we'll just listen for his cab.

After a while you could have heard them forget about that. Winn held his shoulders and arms. I think you're making me pregnant she said like it was necessity's happy event. But that's what I want, Max, she said.

Aren't you supposed to say *testing*, Winn said, or take one? You just want me to talk?

Okay, you want me to say who I want, you or Richard, she said.

But who didn't want to keep what they had or get what they wanted or take away what someone's got, Maximilian thought. Better not to want at all, but who the hell could keep that up.

Winn walked out of the frame, she looked out the window for any color that could stop the eye.

If I had a daisy, I'd have to choose: he loves me, he loves me, Winn said.

He drove around looking for dogs for his film but it was too hot for dogs. Dogs dreaming about running, the chase. Dreams like we have, he thought.

Two months passed.

She said Jesus these jets they set your teeth on edge don't they Max. She lay down on the floor beside him, she bent over him with no shirt on like some movie from France.

Move closer will you Max? Can you sleep? Guess not now.

He picked up the Bolex but she swept his face with her hair, she said I like the way your hand smells. I like to talk into it. Max-i-mi-li-an.

They got in the car—too hot to talk lying down.

Even in black and white you could see the heat. They drove without clothes because who could see them?

Winn said, I peed on the strip, it turned pink.

Years had gone by when he hadn't even touched anyone. He said, have you told Richard yet?

She said, he got radiated, I told you. So it couldn't be his.

She said, do you want a child, Max?

Well, he'd been one, he said; it hadn't been marvelous.

Winn shrugged. But here we are now, all grown up.

They picked Richard up by the Trona U-Wash. Dick wore Winn's tee shirt inside out; it was really Maximilian's shirt. He'd gave her that shirt off his back.

Now that the taxi was clean she, too, wanted to be clean. *Make a clean breast of it.*

She'd tell Dick right now but they'd fallen across his mattress.

But his pillow smelled fresh, he'd turned her on her knees.

Listen, Winn said in her head.

It's hard to believe we've done this a thousand times, Richard said.

Winn remembered all the times.

She liked this small tidy room behind the Trona Car Wash, the submarine rides in the car through the wash like a carnival ride.

She said, remember that time we sold candy apples from that truck where we lived?

I was driving for Blue Bonnet Cab in Ann Arbor, Dick said.

Flint, Winn said. Ah but nothing went too good for Dick. Well, Winn thought, I go good with him.

Dick parted the curtain to make sure the taxi was all right out there. Winn stood with her hands on her hips like she had when she'd still been faithful to him. She'd always said what she wanted to say so she put on her blouse, hugged her arms, but she wouldn't be able to talk about it in no pants.

They drove the back roads though all of the roads were back roads. Wind blew hair from her brow with the windows all down in the clean taxicab. They bought ice cream but they ate it too fast, it gave them that third-eye ache in the head.

At the cistern, she swam belly up for him.

Dick said, you've got guppies in there, I bet.

Yes, she said. At least, one.

Richard smiled sideways at her though it was a bit thin. They tracked sand in the cab, she got the seat all wet.

So let's have a harmonica for the road, Richard said, or some whistling, even.

What would not be a lie to film?
Maximilian cut the movie with scissors and tape while Winn shined the flashlight from beneath. He studied his reels frame by frame like that Zapruder film: Richard in his battleship underpants. Winn on the sand where the dirt road ended, saying we're just small bags of wetness here, Max.

What if he cut what was good, how did he know what that was? But he knew what he'd have liked to watch, if he was the one watching this. He said, turn it off; he said, I don't even like movies that much.

How many times have you said that? Winn said.

Every time.

It barely cooled down at twilight; they'd been thinking of names for the kid.

How about Mojave? Winn said. They laughed but they didn't rule it out. Or Evelyn, my dead sister, Winn said.

Your dead sister, Maximilian said.

All that old trauma-drama, Winn said. That old cornball unhappiness.

He couldn't make out her face in the dark about how she said this.

It can be a man's name too, she said. In England.

They leaned over the black and white strip in his hand: dirty snow, bare-branched trees on the highway to Saint Boniface.

So Max now I made myself sad. Winn wiped a fake tear with the back of her palm. Do you think it's bad luck, a dead person's name for the kid?

What he liked about Winn is she didn't look sad in her soon-to-be motherness. She didn't care about luck, or believe you could figure things out with your brain, or the body, even.

He picked up the film from the floor so they wouldn't slice their bare feet. What he liked about movies is how what gets cut, even more so for that, is still there.

Only asleep is when they remembered what winter was like, thin ice, a cool rain and a grayed-over sky. If they could have collected their wits, they might have imagined a cloud.

We got married in rain in a borrowed blue dress, Richard said. I mean Winn wore the dress.

But weren't they pleased with themselves? Pregnant, and driving a cab, and Winn could be famous a little bit from this movie, she thought, with maybe a little white house in her mind, and look at my belly! she said.

Karl Marx Echs, Rosa Luxemburg Legg, Richard said, trying names for the kid. Soon there'd be no presidents but a child shall lead them, he said. When the revolution comes.

Sometimes he slept in a chair by the door like a guard dog in the yard.

How hot was it? Their brain flickered like film at the end of a reel that went white.

Winn hung a calendar on the wall, though in this heat you barely dared think of a clock. Maximilian tried on a cryptic half-smile when Dick drove off with

Winn in the cab. He knew: Dick took her to eat pickled eggs at the bar.

They'd only been driving around, Richard said, just talking and they must have fallen asleep.

But keep loving each other a lot; that's *good*, Winn, Maximilian thought.

Because why shouldn't she have everything while she walked around like she cradled a small cantaloupe, bought a Mom magazine, washed her hair by moonlight.

Maybe it's raining in Camden, Dick said, or in your Baltimore, Max.

They'd coast down a hill on a sled, wear those mittens with strings that smelled like a dog when they're wet. *Evelyn* sewn in the kid's underpants.

Here wind blew sand everywhere; all that's solid melts into air, Richard said Karl Marx said.

How many things could you say about heat?

The kid'll *hatch* here, reptile eyes with that extra membrane, Maximilian said. Winn had her back turned, he spoke into her shoulders and hair.

She spread cream on her belly, she said where do you get your bad thoughts?

How do you stop a thought?

Outside, bones were found off the highway sometimes: people thought they could hike, they wandered away from their cars. The brown earth blue sky seemed cut from cardboard with an X-acto knife.

Winn said, can you do your thing, Max? Can we just cut to wintertime now?

Not so fast. First he had to film one thousand frames about how they were with each other those months. You think you'd know how you'd act but you wouldn't know how, while Winn went with Dick to talk about what people married for twenty years talked about.

Winn wore her dress with the seams taken out, a light coat for the cold that she couldn't button in a while.

Rain never touched down from the sky; it fell on the Amargosa Range and swept by. Winn put on Dick's muster-out cap, she said time to go, guys.

Dick turned on the Lucky Cab occupied light. Hard rain fell biblically in the lakes that the road had become.

We'll be there in a minute, Dick said.

I could have a child in a minute, Winn said.

Or make one, Dick said.

Maximilian thought about those timelines where humans appeared at five minutes to noon and by noon mankind was civilized.

For an expert at it, how bad could Dick possibly park?

At the desk Richard said, she's our wife. Maximilian held the camera and the pink diaper bag.

Rain softened the walls and they put cups and rags all around to try keeping the new weather out.

If there's no heat, what's the point of the desert? Winn said.

Now Vee slept between Winn and whoever's room she was in.

When is a joke not a joke? She tried stopping herself in the middle of telling Richard: the kid looks like you, Dickie, she said.

It's never just one thing that causes another but still. . . .

In the morning the taxi was gone.

Maybe he just went to Ridgecrest for cab parts, Winn said. To watch twenty-four hours of television.

Maybe he stepped out for cigarettes, Maximilian said, and Winn laughed but only because it was like her to laugh.

She drove to Darwin to check general delivery for a postcard. They rode around looking for him but it was like a dog chasing a car—if it caught it then what?

Should she have said, the kid *doesn't* look like you, Dick?

Maximilian wiped the kid's rosy behind, he waited for Winn with Vee in his lap while she telephoned veterans homes from the bar. Maybe she ordered a drink like a man with a reason for it.

What if she grew troubled and sad and she couldn't be helped? But when she came out she wore a crème de menthe smile. But you love me, she said, but she wore the boots Richard had left.

He wondered what it would be like without Winn —cars going by on Route 189—would he keep filming that? Sometimes at night cars drove past the motel, headlights sweeping the bed. He pictured he finished the movie and lived by himself. He kept a hand someplace on Winn while she slept.

They took rides in the car.

Winn said, it's been twelve good months, Max. It's Dick's turn to be happy, Winn said.

He'd planned on making a short and sweet movie about this Christmas and the next ten Christmases. When New Years Day came, he'd film that: you'd see all the cars driving drunk.

She said, anyhow, Max, you've always been fine by yourself.

But aren't we fine, too? But he didn't say this.

Why had affection always felt so odd to him? People said they craved it. He used to, before, from sad country songs about how to be sad when he drank.

She said, we'll be all right, have a little faith, Max.

Rainwater had filled up the dishes and cups. He filmed that and the room's underwatery light, the same dumb things he always had. He gave her a ride to the airport but he wouldn't get out of the car, she'd have to catch her plane by herself. It was the only one moment of power over her he had. He sat in the car and she leaned in the window with Vee on her hip.

Dick's anchor is only an anchor tattoo, Maximilian said.

She backed up a step. An airplane obliterated whatever she said. He wanted to film her walking away, across the white parking space lines. If there had been wind and rain, it could have blown into her hair and her dress for effect but the day was unambiguously perfect.

I'll call you a million times, Winn said, but he kind of doubted it.

He got out and got corny with Vee for a while. They stood in the lot and Winn said, now don't drive like you're wanting to crash.

He opened his palms like don't be ridiculous. What could they say next, goodbye? They said that. He got in the car and rolled up the window; the cool winter sun warmed his hands.

He sat in the car for a while. He didn't want to go home because what if he liked it, then what had he had? Or would this be the part where he mooned around taking pictures of sad little flowers.

At the motel coffee shop he ate two grilled cheese sandwiches. Werner hung himself at the Sunspot Airporter Motel. Last time they met Werner had brought him Freud's Gessamelte Werke. Those long German nouns are like train cars across you know where, Werner said.

In Darwin he cut out some parts of the movie he probably should have kept.

The phone rang in the telephone booth.

Winn said, you've never seen pink like my waitress's uniform, Max, but the Peter Pan collar is cool and the silly white hat. Like a sailor's cap. She shouldn't, perhaps, have said that.

But he'd lived nearby, he knew what Camden was like. At this time of year snow wouldn't stop; if you ran the *hey baby* gauntlet you'd come to a little crack park where Winn might have pushed Vee's stroller along because the kid ought to know what grass was.

So how's Vee, Winn, he said.

She sleeps in a box by our bed and you'll laugh: Dick now eats M&M's.

Okay I'm laughing he said. He blew on his hand, wished he smoked. At least Winn didn't put Richard on, she didn't ask how his movie was coming along.

She said, I like it here, Max, like she had to be mean to him now. Does that make you too sad?

He said, but you're calling me, Winn.

Behind her the traffic went by. She said I wanted to Max so don't say things like that.

It would have been cold where she stood. Though you couldn't see it, he'd been writing her name on the glass.

No one had wanted his Werner film. This bar Werner propped him up at had this moviola machine: For a handful of quarters you could watch a strip show, a Chinese fire drill, you could see the bulls run at Pamplona again and again.

Werner's pressed orchestra shirts: he saved the cardboard shirt-backs. He'd tossed a rug in the folded down back of the blue Country Squire so the kid slid around hairpin turns. He let Maximilian steer with one hand, he let go—aren't you going to grab the wheel, kid?

He'd played piano in a Friedrichstrasse bar; one evening Claude Debussy came in.

Later, a season of cheese sandwiches, dust in the black Kiwi paste. All night the oboe girl wept, the trombone cut her wrist. Werner's girls with their violin cases like small caskets across their legs. He drove with the windows rolled down, sheets from Der Rosenkavalier floated out. Some of those brides didn't even know how to carry a kid.

He carried a cloth handkerchief, he had monarchist tendencies.

He didn't want to be good but he was afraid about punishment.

He wore colorful shirts with wide stripes.

I can smell the booze coming off of you kid, Werner said at the airport motel.

Did you eat, kid? There's some good salami in the fridge. I'm getting married again. Anyhow, it's not a crime, it's an institution, Werner said.

The orchestra roamed, he wouldn't be staying for long.

This salami's from Bavaria, kid. He cut careful slices, he ate off the knife, wiped the blade on a folded napkin.

He talked about killing himself. Maximilian waited him out. Soon Werner would be both dead and alive, he'd be Schrödinger's cat.

Not every musician *likes* music, he'd said.

Come right now, Winn said. He stood in the telephone booth in Darwin, happy and ambivalent.

He drove over water somewhere, he passed Caves of Mystery Ahead. He'd forgot there were so many trees, even in parts of Texas.

You could think things through driving *past*: like Flaubert with his book without words, he'd wanted a movie without images. Freud said the successful dream is the unrecalled dream; still, he tried to remember everyone he ever loved—a short but exhausting list.

So what could he show about Camden that you couldn't already guess?

I thought you won't want to miss Richard dying, Winn said. Her room was too small for too many thoughts but it had a window to take pictures from. He'd never abandoned his movies for long. That's how his love was—there was always that other love.

They walked in the little drug park, they swung Vee by her hands. Did you know he was sick when you left? Maximilian said.

Winn picked up Vee to disguise that she had. She said, the event didn't belong to you, Max.

But you changed your mind, you must have missed whatever about me you missed, Maximilian said.

Winn almost smiled. I let Richard decide, it's his show now, Max.

The hospital looked dirty white like the snow on the ground.

You'd think there'd be tubes but Richard was eating a sandwich in bed. It's going to come up anyhow, Richard said.

Maximilian opened the drapes for more light but he filmed just the curtain with blue and white stripes, how snow came in and dripped off the ledge. He looked out the window, Winn waiting down there. I used to think it would be good if the people I cared for were dead, then I wouldn't have to worry about them, he said. He put on Dick's cap, Richard held out his hand with the sandwich in it. Here, you want some? They shared it.

What would Evelyn think she remembered about those days, later on? Her mother's husband descending the hospital fire escape in a gown. Winn drove the getaway cab, Dick lifted Vee to his chest, his arms were like bird skeletons in the Natural History Museum.

One day there'll be no one who even remembers this taxi, Dick said.

That's right, take the long view, Winn said.

At least there'll be nobody left to be sad about you, Maximilian said.

This short-daylight month—in the movie, he won't draw it out.

Who wants to see one more thing anyhow? Maximilian said.

Well I wouldn't mind, Richard said. He'd been trying to smoke, lit a bent Tareyton.

They rode three in the front plus the kid like they couldn't stand being apart. Maximilian held the camera on Dick, he said, what's dying like? There was ten seconds left on the reel so he just had to ask.

Richard coughed, then he laughed: you're an ass.

They drove by Harleigh Lake, by the cemetery, by mistake. Trees leaned over graves in the rain.

Oh brother, Winn said.

I'll pick out a spot now, Dick said.

Winn rolled her eyes, she fed him those small chocolate donuts he liked that came six to a cellophane pack. He unfolded a government paper, he said, see, here's the pension you'll get. Winn made a big paper snowball from it, she rolled down the window, tossed it. Don't be stupid about this, Dick said.

Later on, who'd tell Vee these stories from Camden? Your fathers rode you with their fares, read you impossible books and Karl Marx while they parked. The river reflected the sky while everyone strolled you for hours. Go ask Max, he'll show you this movie he made—Dick tasting your Gerber's mashed peas, Max wearing your bib on his head, and look, there's that old taxicab.

In a film you can cut stuff or try something else but in real life they buried Richard.

What's good about Camden is it got stuck in its past, it had union stickers on cars. Winn put a notice in the paper for old Navy guys and some came, and a guy from the merchant marine and a couple of taxi drivers brought their hacks.

Rain blew in brief gusts. Winn wore a scarf but she took it off when it got wet. She looked like Jackie O. when they buried Jack, Maximilian thought. The wind blew Winn's coat and some notes she wrote about Dick. She'd bought a black dress and she took off her coat in the cold because it would be a shame not to show it. Someone who was drunk whistled and stopped. The merchant marine held Vee tenderly, put his hat on her head.

Up there—though there was no up there, really, just a rise by the grave—Winn said, I knew him the whole time I was married to him. Some construction equipment went by on the road so you could hear only pieces.

Would you like to say a few words, Max? Winn said.

He was a Communist and an atheist, Maximilian said.

He was a good husband mostly, Winn said. Well his intentions were good. Who knows what his intentions were, she said. Wind blew the paper in her hand. The merchant marine said why did she bother with notes if she's not reading them?

Not everybody had tattoos back then, Winn said, so that's why I married him. The mourners stepped foot to foot in the cold. Winn had made sandwiches in a sack by her feet but they couldn't have known about that. She touched the rain on her cheeks. He was a good guy when he was around, he was probably good when he wasn't she said. She laughed at herself. Well I loved him, she said. Somebody clapped a few times. She picked up the sack. From up there she said, I made you fellas some tuna fish sandwiches.

If Maximilian had put in his movie that he'd take the kid and she'd stay, she wouldn't have believed it. But also she wasn't as sad as she thought she'd be with Dick dead. And she couldn't sleep with Max now anyhow with dead Richard spooking around. She opened the window, looked down. Dick's driving around us like our guilty conscience, she said.

I didn't think you had one, in a good way, Maximilian said.

Winn laughed. She said, why am I laughing? I'm sad.

How to be happy is don't do things that make you unhappy, Maximilian said. As if he ever didn't do that. And she didn't want his advice, or him trying to get her unsad or even just hanging around—she'd just *had* a husband.

He watched her watching the street like Richard might really show up.

You can't see me good if you're always looking at me, Winn said. She lit one of Dick's cigarettes. If you went home you could finish your movie, she said.

People had left him because of that stupid Bolex. He used to let things go away so that he could keep them: he ruined the *now* to have *then*.

She said, I've never been all alone, Max, I want to see what it's like without you. Anyone. She was lining up reasons like there was even such a thing. She pictured herself smoking and knocking around in Camden; she could get used to it. She said, Darwin's not so bad for a kid.

He would have stood closer to her but she kept that cigarette smoke between them. You want me to take her, he said, like a fact he had to double check.

She wasn't supposed to think like this, she supposed, but she was: she loved Vee but she trusted Max more than herself. It's not a moral decision, she said.

The pipes ticked but no heat came out. They wore every coat, they could see each other's breath in the cold tenement. If Max had Vee, she thought, she'd have to go back to him. She warmed Vee's bottle on the stove, squirted milk on her wrist to test it.

Rain caused the landscape to change or maybe his mind shifted it. He'd already called her from X and X and X and he hadn't blamed her for a thing.

Vee all right? Winn said.

She's eating sand right this minute, he said.

Right, she said. Why do people talk anyhow?

He called back.

She laughed. My mouth's full of M&M's, Max. She was like Vee: what she thought was the same as she was.

She said I almost wrote a postcard but I tore it up in my mind.

He was trying to open a pack of string cheese while he held the phone to Vee's ear so she wouldn't forget who Winn was.

When I was a kid my dad stalled the car in the Callahan Tunnel, Winn said. He walked out for help while I stayed in the car while the traffic behind it backed up. She said, I kind of feel like that now.

She promised to call him at six at the gas station phone because how much change could he carry around?

Winn said, who can love anybody enough for all these telephone calls?

It's our own desire we love, Maximilian said but this was only some idea he'd read.

Winn said, funny the small things you miss and you didn't realize you missed them, like I can't look at a cab or a kid or married people for God's sake.

That's a lot not to see, Maximilian said. Behind her he thought he could hear the snow fall.

Nothing feels inevitable, now, she said, but is that good or bad?

He peeled string cheese from the pack, he said hold on, I'll put Vee on.

I've been reading Dear Abby's cool-eyed advice. I've been watching the small weedy lot where three sisters play princesses. They all want to be kissed awake.

My postcard:

I bet it's always raining in your mind! That girl singer you made a movie about, you don't know but I saw the whole thing, I drove all the way to Ridgecrest to see it. Did you know it costs $34 to rent?

That singer still dead who sang in the echoey places where she sounded better, she said. That girl who might deign a stray press of her hip. "A hundred sad songs from her songbook of sad-song reasons," you said.

Even then, Max, I see you were fond of your facts: Baltimore, dirty grass, pigeons grey like the rain and they fought in the rain on the dirty sidewalk.

And your reindeer-flap hat: you made yourself ridiculous! Your pint in your pocket that clanged against newspaper racks, and you'd have to quit drinking you said if you wanted to finish the film, and then you were sure if you wanted to end it you'd have to start drinking again.

But what you really like, still, are all the happy accidents—when you cut off her head, when a bus crossed in front of the lens.

Well she might have called you her Sorrows of Werther but she was the one who opened a window and jumped.

How you love someone dead: it's never the same with anyone else after that, is it, Max.

So you can't mind I can't sing; I don't care you can't sail, after all, no tattoos, and it's true that the note that arrives is the one that's not sent: this card to myself on the fridge with the fruity magnets until I throw it out.

He'd been driving in rain on Mud Road, his wipers smeared rain and insects. He stopped at the gas station phone to call Winn.

She said, I still miss a ride in a van but she was no free bird, or girl anymore with the highway's shoulder to lean on.

Does Vee miss me? Winn said.

Maximilian shrugged though Winn couldn't see that. He said, she hasn't mentioned you yet.

That's a joke, Winn, he said.

Sometimes how to talk to you best is to stay off the telephone, Max. Sunspots flared on the sun, the connection got bad, she said gotta go, Max.

Vee stuck her hand in dust motes from the projector's lamp. They watched Winn in the film on the wall holding her hair from her face, drinking water from the tap. He made a duck silhouette, a barking dog over Winn's head. I'll teach you to cut film, he told Vee, you have the small hands for it.

He slept in his clothes because what was a reason for taking them off? He shaved because he thought Vee should see a guy shave. He looked at his watch but it wasn't time to call yet.

They drove over bad roads that dipped, one hand on the wheel, the other across the front seat to hold Vee. They cowboyed around the salt flats, he said we're Bonnie and Clyde. If Clyde brought his camera along, if Bonnie was tiny and fat. If Clyde had a wife not a wife in Camden.

A late spring rain fell at the end of the road that washed out. He said what do we do now? Rain slanted through the headlights, he danced Vee on his lap. You don't know, it's okay not to know, he said. It'll be a long time until you might even believe that.

It was time to go back, clean Vee up and cut film and call Winn. He looked at his watch, it had stopped, he'd forgot to wind it.

How many calls had she made in a couple of months? Enough to empty her tip jar. In Darwin by now tiny flowers were already pushing up shoots, they were making a stand.

She pictured herself in the film as she went about in Camden, her pea-green coat black and white on the wall of the room at the Pending motel. Sometimes she talked to Richard out loud. Even with everyone walking around she told Vee what was what.

Winn put on her waitress's coffee shop cap not unlike a sailor's cap. She buttoned her blouse with her name in blue thread on the heart. Some greenery pushed through concrete, rain washed away snow, her ankles got wet crossing Van Horn to Main, her feet would stay damp through her shift.

She rowed on the lake with a guy who came in for breakfasts, mister one-soft-boiled-egg she called him. You seem like a happy person, he said. Sure, why not? Anyway she hadn't told him that her husband died or that she had a kid. She didn't tell him that part of her mourning was *this*.

But this was more like an old song that was better remembered than played. Or not even that. She'd never been fond of the mind, it was for people like Max who made something from it. In her own head her brain only talked to itself.

Trees hung over the lake so you couldn't see the graves anyway.

Max should have got this on film: this breakfast person's soft-boiled kiss, how she laughed, shook her head, said tomorrow your eggs are on me, so to speak. Unfertilized!

Why had she wanted to moon around Dick anyhow, chew sand over Max, not have Vee in her arms? Because no one could kiss like a sailor before his ship sailed. If thinking was needed, she knew who to call and she knew where Vee was. She rowed toward the shore, she was a stronger rower than anyone.

He liked carrying Vee through Darwin, he liked being watched carrying Vee by the women in town. He felt like some heroic version of them, the police girl, the librarian. The woman who came to Darwin to collect Indian artifacts. If you asked he'd have said he wasn't interested but men always are.

An early spring rain, then it would be the end of the rain.

She seemed practical with her rocks in boxes with smaller boxes inside. They shared an onion and butter sandwich on a bench by the gunnery range underneath the loud jets. Her name was—he couldn't make it out. I want to be in your movie she said. Everyone did even if they said they didn't. He took thirty meters of her in her archeology pants.

She held Vee in the street as if pretending Vee was hers. People remembered Winn, though, even though Darwin wasn't a kind of place where you'd say anything about that.

Hand me that wrench; she'd been trying to fix his car that had broken again; he'd been showing her interesting rocks by the Dry Lake turnout. That early spring rain wasn't the last, after all. They'd put Vee in the back.

What do we do now? she asked.

She took off her pants that got wet crawling under the frame, her blue underpants like a damp darker skin.

She said, we could just use our hands, then it wouldn't mean anything.

He knew better than that. He said what would be the point of it then? The rain on the windshield patterned her blouse but it wasn't yet too late to stop, then Vee woke up crying in back and he lifted Vee up. He tried the ignition, it caught.

Now you're happy, she said.

Who'd have guessed West Texas had trees, weeping willows, even. These bus guys said things like check out the tall girl in back; like, what's up with that sailor hat? She put her fingers to her lips, she flashed a ring she'd bought almost only for this.

In back of the bus she was peeling a sandwich and dunking the bread in coffee with sugar and milk. Three days in, her dress in a brown paper bag, she wanted only to empty her pockets on top of a dresser somewhere.

At night people fucked on the bus.

Oh Richard, nobody's running toward anyone slowly with flowers, she thought.

She needed to look at some water for him so she got off the dog and climbed in a taxi, she spent her coins riding and seeing what he would have seen. She slept by the banks of a river, she slept through every departing Greyhound. If Max was around with his camera, she'd be a picture, she thought.

She woke up confused because Max wasn't there, Dick was dead.

She counted her coins, there wasn't enough for a choice about what to do next. What if Dick floated downstream and she floated with him but that was so far from her style and he had that anchor tattoo and she wouldn't swim after him, after all.

The weather held out, she got weeds in her hair from the woods where she slept. *Oh Richard*, sure—but did she really want him ghosting around, wooing maidens from the banks?

She took off her blouse and her pants and washed them. Nothing to do but think about Max reading Schopenhauer in her panties and bra—she laughed out loud—she meant *she* was in them, not him.

Maximilian liked jokes like that, she could call him right now: Richard said you should bring me some flowers she'd say although it was really her wish. She put on her dress to look nice for her telephone call: come and get me she said.

She had toilet paper, the weather stayed warm, she'd wait for his airplane to land. A few days went by, but she didn't mind, much.

Outside the perimeter fence, Winn wore the blanket she'd rolled herself in, her dress with some blue still in it. She said Look at you, Vee, and you, Max. She said, Aw, your old car!

She wanted to drive but he needed to rest, to decide what came next.

Maximilian kept an eye out for Werner at the airport motel. He looked in the fridge for sausages, a clasp knife or iced slivovic.

So did you finish your movie? Winn said.

He stared out the sliding glass door as if The End was out there. He turned up his palms. It's too short, hardly anything happens, he said.

The stray yellow weeds he'd picked thirty miles back died quick in the toothbrushing glass. She'd forgot to take off her ring; or you could say, on purpose, *not forgot.*

She counted her change. Do we have enough to go back? Do you want to? Winn asked.

He stood at the sliding glass door, go back in which direction? he said.

I mean, Winn said, go *ahead.*

He picked up his camera from the nightstand. The Bolex missed having you in it, he said.

She thought all her Camden woozing around had been—what? Vee cried so they took her outside to watch the small planes wobble in.

I feel bad that I want one to crash, Maximilian said.

Yeah, I always take it right back when I wish that, Winn said. She held Vee, then he did, then she did. He filmed Winn waving Vee's arms, nothing brilliant, but he didn't care about that. The West Texas wind blew their clothes and their hair and Winn shielded Vee's eyes against it.

running toward
Slowly

East or west? Because who could stay in Texas?

They sat in the car, Vee in Maximilian's lap. Once he'd been a little famous but not now and he'd worn his old camera out. Darwin was nothing but hot; he'd used it all up.

So why *not* Texas?

I've been through here once, he said. You don't do that twice unless you mean to stop.

Oh God, Winn said but she didn't really mind. She opened the map, she said, where do you want to go, kid?

Vee put the map in her mouth and Winn touched the wet spot with her thumb.

Magnet, Texas drew them.

Maximilian set up the tent. Just because here we are now doesn't mean it's forever, he said.

Well, Dick, so much for your ocean, she thought.

No, not forever, she said. I sure know about that.

A postcard: How is Magnet like Darwin? There are no interesting cactuses, Dick. If I have to live in a tent, shouldn't I have to marry him, Dick? What happened to *old* Bedford, she wrote.

When Dick sailed he hadn't cared if she didn't send him long letters like other wives sent. When they moved, again, her waitress's uniform's color went from Annapolis pink to New Bedford salmon.

She'd pictured Dick's life at sea: men ironing creases in slacks, a shipful of men who knew how to sew a button on, mend a rip. "I'm watching the coastline for you—naval gazing," she wrote. She could hardly wait for him to get home so he could swab the linoleum. He'd show her his latest tattoo, teach her sailor chess and maybe a new bedroom trick.

Mostly I miss kissing he said in the postcard he sent.

The candle made her shadow lunge on the tent in Magnet. She made an eagle, a dog, a giant spider on the slanted canvas. She took Maximilian's wrist, she pulled his hand toward the Bolex. Come on, Max, make your movie, she said. She made her bird fly, her dog bark, her bug crawl. Though what if he got it on film, still it would last just as long as the candle stayed lit. Or about as long as a kiss.

In Magnet there's a Billie Neal Road and a New Billie Neal Road. A cemetery, the Acheson-Topeka train tracks.

She only stopped by the house because it was one of the only houses. She was just walking by, here where people only rode horses, drove trucks.

So you just knock? The door halfway open.

Billy Neal's canvases leaned on a broken-backed chair, a workbench.

My grandmothers founded this town, Billy said, rubbed his face, rubbing out last night's alcohol.

Winn stood there, there being no place to sit.

How can you paint, your hands shaking like that?

Long sand-colored swoops, some kind of abstract Texas.

Billy Neal shrugged—"Billy," he signed them, she saw, although he's a grown man.

She'd only gone inside because she had the idea Maximilian needed a new thing to film. And she always needed someone to deflect too much togetherness. To refract them back on themselves. But she wouldn't get into all that.

You're camped on my land, Billy said.

Passing through. Vagabondage, she said. It's just our gypsy tent.

When Dick didn't die they sold candied apples from the truck. Driving around, she knew how to plan a route, read a map. They pulled the tin trailer all through the Pacific Northwest, slept in each other's stickiness, their red love like thick blood but sweet. Apples gone mushy inside though she still believed she could leave any time if she didn't think how those apples might click if you passed a wand over them.

Billy Neal looked her up and down.

What? Want to paint me? she said, but she didn't mind getting looked at.

I don't paint real things, Billy said.

Winn shrugged. Well what's real, she said, stupid because she knew what.

But you could come down where we're parked, I'll make you a bologna sandwich, she said.

Billy Neal's mouth held a laugh. I suppose that's one incentive, he said.

It's kind of a joke not a joke: how is Magnet like Darwin. What they had in the past, what they have to be careful about: the man and the woman and somebody else.

Like their car broke down so they had to use somebody else to put things in motion.

Like she carries Vee the seventeen miles to look at the ocean. Sometimes she catches a ride. Funny, when Dick was around, she didn't miss the sea; he'd carried it on his skin; his anchor: it pulled him.

With Vee in her arms she'd walk, cop a ride in whatever passed. Wanting to go there trumped being afraid of who she got in beside. Anyway sometimes she walked all the way, it took more than four hours. The sky could be delicate, harsh. Not an unkind road, the odd tire rim, the snakeskin.

Even if she left at dawn she wouldn't be able to walk home at night. The snakeskin means snakes. A scary car ride. Someone would have to come looking for her and know looking's needed.

Small stones, sea grass, sparse tufts of weeds like torn beards. The shoreline would take on the quarter moon's shape if she stayed. You'd have to burn every weed to make even a palm-sized fire, if the weeds weren't too damp, if she'd thought to bring a match.

Billy Neal coming down Billie Neal Road, he had paint on his hands. The car radio turned to Texas.

How did Billy know where to come in his uncolored Volkswagen bug? Well he knows these parts, like where the road ends for instance and why someone would want to take it.

Vee's hand in Winn's the kid tottering on cool sand in the bright overcast. Winn saying, how did you know where we went?

Dust devils from Billy Neal's car spiraling behind them. Yeah that's something isn't it, Billy says.

Billy Neal lit a cigarette. Winn fanned the smoke from Vee's face. Billy put it out.

Winn had to laugh. You lit it so you could do that, she said.

The two Billie Neal streets like a tuning fork up ahead and the tent between them. Winn thought let's not go back yet and he guessed. They stopped for powdered donuts.

You don't have to live like this, Billy said. He'd lit another cigarette.

Live like what? Winn wiped the sugar off her mouth. Name a thing you think I want I don't have, she said. She thought it wasn't quite what he meant.

Not a tent for instance, Billy said. He blew smoke in her eyes. Think about what your husband should do for you, girl, Billy said. What he wants for himself.

Now Winn wished he'd drive, get some air in this car. He believes in the redistribution of wealth, Winn said. Billy's antimacassars on armchairs, for instance. Furniture of generations.

I could give him the money to finish his film, Billy said.

Billy Neal in his Hawaiian print shirt, his blond blown-dry hair—wasn't he too obvious. Winn laughed: Billy made her nervous. She liked it.

Anyway, he's not my husband, she said.

Billy drank from his flask. The temptation would be to find me *humorous*, Billy said.

Winn put a donut in her mouth. Or to think Maximilian a fool, she said.

Billy drank from his flask. And how am I getting *you* wrong?

Winn put another donut in her mouth. She smiled around it; she said when she could, to think I'm more complicated.

Billy drank, he passed her the flask. Oh, I don't think that, darling, he said.

Billy Neal's pores, even with every window rolled down, smelled like every room Maximilian sweated out alcohol in. He stared through the buggy windshield at the landscape made for drinking.

Your wife's settled in nicely, Billy said. Echs and Billy Neal bumping over bad roads looking for road signs to kill with Billy's .38.

Not my wife, Maximilian said. Winn in Billy's soft shirts, the wind blown up her crossed legs by the tent.

Billy aimed the pistol as he steered. I could give you the money to finish your movie, he said, shot a hole through a hole in a fence.

You notice the moves when a gun's waved around in a small moving car. Billy sloshed bourbon around the bologna sandwich in his mouth. I'll give you the money if you let me have Winn, he said. Pushed the gun into Maximilian's hand.

Vee shouldn't live in the dirt, Winn had said. Vee needs more than a tin basin bath.

Winn the stealer of afternoons at Billy Neal's house. Sure, wasn't it obvious once you knew what you're looking at. Like those trick pictures where you see the rabbit then duck, stairs that also go upside down, the beautiful girl or the witch—and now Winn liked Lynyrd Skynyrd and not Leonard Cohen, she said.

Maximilian aimed at the nothing out there, the grip hot, the gun heavier than he'd thought.

Well, you'll have to ask her, he said.

Billy drank, he spilled some on his shirt with toucans. I have, friend.

The gun jumped like a wild thing you shouldn't pick up; how they say it *discharged*, that was right. The car swerved.

It went off, Maximilian said and he couldn't help laugh, placed the gun carefully on the seat between them.

Billy put his hand over it. Next time, keep your eyes open, he said.

Winn held Vee, glad for it, but not as happy as Maximilian thought she should be. He wanted to ask her how much she'd really missed Vee, and him, in Camden. Like there was a scale with guilt's counterweight that might be appropriate. Like now she had to prove it.

Summer! Jesus! Winn said. Her wet bathing suit left a stain on the hood of the tan Volkswagen. Hot wind blew from all directions. Their brains gone to mush in the tent or else whited out in the outer brightness. While up at the house Billy strummed his guitar. From afar it sounded like insects.

And didn't she feel like she'd thrown in her lot with the most careless part of herself—like some poor second-hand tragedy although she had no fate she'd admit. If she saw it clear there'd be only the scrubby outskirts of Magnet, some fools standing around in the shimmering heat.

Do you even care about this? she said. Her waving hand took it in: where they lived, herself, the kid, him.

He took Vee from Winn. More than he could say: that was the problem. He held Vee and had hopes for

Vee; you were supposed to, for a kid. He could see good and bad things in the future of Vee. She'd be smart, not so bohemian. She still had time to add and subtract sadnesses.

Well then, Max, Winn said, his name like he used to like her to say it. Like something important was going to come next. But no. That was it.

He wanted to step in a shade that was cool, comforting, but there was none like that here and you couldn't step into the shade of yourself.

Vee pointed at their long shapes, what's *that*? Who's *that*?

Winn laughed. Shook her head.

Life and no escape, Maximilian said, though he meant it in a happy way, throwing out that Zen rope with nothing at either end.

She'd overslept by mistake on purpose. Billy's nine rooms, she slept in any room Billy didn't.

Candles on petals in bowls: they'd been burning all night: Maximilian could see them from the tent. Winn sleeping in very few clothes, all the windows open.

She was drinking water from the tap. You've been thinking how bad could it be, you've been thinking about it, Billy said.

Winn wrapped herself in the curtain fluffed with 3 a.m. wind; you could see her footprints, if it hadn't been night, from the tent to the house. She drank a little from Billy's bourbon.

No sex idea goes unthought.

She'd come down anytime, right?

And we'd be doing this because why? Winn said. She should have been mad because it was a joke she and Billy began about Max, about poorness and circumstances. Pretending what could they do about it?

Her shadow across every window, Winn holding the candle with Billy behind her, his gun in the car.

Another sick guy to take care of, Winn said watching Billy's hands shake and the alcohol sweats. You think I'm the girl who'll drag you from bars, she told him, clean you up. Though she didn't think he thought that.

Yeah you might even fuck me sober, Billy said.

She kept her distance. Such a large man: she could take his weight though, she could want to be crushed or there'd be large stumbling accidents. Well it could happen, you could never tell what people would do or you could but what's the difference if you did.

Sound carried further at night all the way from the house.

And that's why I love him Winn said as the candle went out with the wind or a breath.

Billy gone drinking in town, they guessed they'd hear his car. They watched pieces of the movie on the wall. Though he'd said he wouldn't show it, but it had Winn in it when she was still only unfaithful to somebody else.

It's clever, Winn said, how you made us more better and worse than ourselves.

How Winn drove how Dick died, Dick saying in Akron we had a dog grooming salon though they'd only had the plan.

If I see it enough, I'll believe that's what really happened, Winn said.

It's a movie, he said, not a lie detector test.

In Billy Neal's house Winn led Maximilian up the stairs by his wrist. You're not supposed to be lonely she said. He smiled behind her. But he was.

What if Vee woke up but Winn took off her clothes to be scared naked in Billy's house. She hoped dirt would rub from their wrists and ankles on Billy's powder-blue sheets. Sweat, she hoped.

Romance in daylight, she said. What if I get pregnant again?

Then at least Vee won't ever be lonely, he said, as if any people could help that. Like they didn't cause it. Outside you could see their footprints and Billy's and Vee's from the tent.

Where do the legs go, insider or out I forget, Maximilian said.

We'll have to ask Billy, Winn said.

With someone you've been with it's always comparing and then he forgot to do that.

Phew Winn said, that was good though they never talked about it. She drank from Billy's bourbon. Am I wider since I had the kid?

Maybe even wiser, he said.

He leaned out the window, Billy's loud radio on. He liked half a song. Piece of My Heart, half of Whole Lotta Love. It sounded better the first six hundred times he heard it. When he believed it. Well, almost. No, he did. He must have.

Any two ways out of town, he can tell what's there by sunlight moonlight headlights. Soon he'll be able to feel his way down the road through the Volkswagen's tires. Gas tank water tank storage shed. What trash lies where, abandoned between the speedometer checks.

He's been driving with Vee aimlessly, uncamera-eyed and uncamera-handed. Who can see even one thing without turning it into a thought? Maybe your mom, kid, he said. Still, he should have been making pictures of Vee; soon the kid's memory machine would begin. Billy Neal's haunted house, the stiff scratch of her father's green tent. Shouldn't Vee have proof about it. The bright signal fire by the ocean that Winn organized for a guy named Dick Legg.

This small round-backed car with the smell that all Volkswagens have, would Vee even remember this part?

Vee unseatbelted, just one more crime in Texas. He pulled her into his lap. Here you steer. He took her hand out of the ashtray; so when're you going to get pierced? A ring in your belly, you'll say fuck you dad.

Vee's hands under his on the wheel. If you're going to drive watch the road, you drive like your mother, he said.

He rested his chin on Vee's head. Can't you spy on her and *report*? Yeah I wouldn't answer me either, he said.

Maximilian parked, took his camera out. Which parts are made up? The filmed evidence—was it just a habit: another season when he'd make even the weather a witnessed event. Because that's what he did.

He explained it to Vee in his head, as if she could make more sense of it than he had.

Does she still love me, kid? I know—you can't say.

Except in the movie, he could. If you watch it enough you'll think that's what really happened.

Between where the Billie roads ran they were firing Billy's bigger gun. It spattered bullets. There'd be no marksmanship.

You don't know her at all, do you, Max? Billy said.

He meant Winn. Somehow she'd got into this.

Everything was mostly a mystery once, Maximilian said.

Like dusk, when objects may appear closer than you thought. The line in the sand they'd been shooting behind got scuffed.

Maximilian had the gun. They were taking out Billy's stepvan, everything he ever drove lay around all shot up. The hot air concussed. No birds and whatever crawled, stopped.

All this noise for Winn who might be hearing it in her late afternoon languidness. Tinkling glass: a wind chime. A Winn charm. Maximilian laughed.

Concentrate, Billy said.

Winn used to smell like warm water poured over her head and then bandages, then like Vee, but now she smelled like Billy's bath salts. Billy's man-perfume. Aramis.

Werner used to splash it around, salt rings under the arms of his tux. He would have loved this, he killed everyone in his brain all the time.

You got to yawn wide when you shoot that thing, Billy said. Pop your ears, swallow hard. Clear your head.

Anything could look like anything in the smoky twilight. Billy Neal's pumpkinhead.

Maximilian aimed at the winning of Winn although she wasn't, probably, *lost.*

The gun in the hand's got a mind of its own in your head, Billy said.

You had to make yourself pry your fingers off.

Cards on the table, he said. Billy said things like that. Being Texan. No ass like a Tex-ass. Still, she wanted to help him: he didn't not need any help, he was dying too fast.

You could go anywhere, Billy, she said.

Could he, though? Wind blew Billy's grandmother's curtain around. Winn's white dress rode up in the night's dirty heat in the bed.

Magnet's made you stupid, Winn said. His boxers with Texas and hearts. Billy puking around the creosote bush where Max buried the trash. The hair on his belly sweated.

Too, he was shorter in bed—it made Winn smile that she had to smile down and him brave enough to look up. Except they were lying down now. His hand on himself and the other hand on her leg.

I'd be kind, Billy said.

You can't even keep a straight face about it, Winn said, but nicely because she liked not liking him. His wallet with cigarette burns on the dresser with bills. For instance, she liked that.

She stood carefully, dizzy, tilted. You could just give me the money, she said.

Look, it's turning you on, Billy said.

Winn laughed but she did feel warm—hot! Well I'm not embarrassed about it, she said.

Billy sticking out in a streak of moonlight.

What's worse, if we do it and I give you money, or we don't and I give you the money, he said.

We do and you don't would be something, Winn said. If she stayed it would happen like weather happens. She looked him over. So we won't. Good, she said.

The candle went out and the moon behind clouds— ah, but who didn't want to be bad—but she already knew her way down in the dark to the tent.

Winn coming down from the house with her white dress aflutter all night: so Max shouldn't look at her like what?

She walked down where their poverty lived. The Marx book torn up on the floor, Max down there beside it.

So, Vee got at it, she said. To spare him.

Yeah, sure, Vee did it, he said.

She got down beside him. Oh Max, she said, you've been *sad*, you've been *hurt*, I've been *underhanded*. One of them would be, or had been, perhaps.

What good is Marx anyhow? Maximilian said.

Winn took Vee in her arms. But we're still broke though, right?

He took Vee from Winn. Are we, then?

She reached out for the kid. Don't be so happy about it, she said.

Vee ran around picking up Marx, she knew not to knock over the candles for light, the Coleman.

Man, though, I could be giving this up, Maximilian said. The poorness.

Me too, Winn said, I could have. Then she lifted her dress, she dangled the Volkswagen keys she took out from her tan underpants. Smells like teen spirit, she said.

He laughed but what was he laughing about? We could just *walk* away, Winn, he said.

The flatness, the flag of Texas, the bareness. Sure but we'll take the car. I can't stand any more nothing, Winn said.

He looked toward the house. There wasn't nothing up there, but they had only nothing to argue about. He put the Bolex in the trunk which was really up front, which was what they had to pack. She kicked out the pole, the tent fell on its knees behind them. He started the car, she held Vee on her lap. The Madonna, Winn said, and the child, and you're still a Communist, man.

toward you

They drove on a road that went on so long it scared them. When he was a kid, he and Werner would leave like this. Cold. Dead of night. The diaspora of hope Werner said like he said things like that. Though now it was warm, almost dawn.

He won't be looking for us, will he, Winn, Maximilian said.

Let's just cross a state line, she said. This is how it used to be, she just went anywhere.

Where's the bandana'd dogs, the tie-dyed harmonicas, Maximilian thought.

Everyplace I ever went, I wanted to live there, he said.

And I left them, Winn said.

Either way you get regrets, if you're the kind to get them, Maximilian said. The road turned north and east; he hadn't said why go this way, or where.

Winn touched his back because she could see his mind. So, Baltimore, then, she said. She couldn't help smile at her intuition. It's only fair because I got to go to Camden, she said.

He and Werner would rush from the Tuscan Motel or the Hotel Seville, though there wasn't even a map about Spain in the town they'd just left.

In Baltimore everyone struggles with summer and autumn and winter and spring, Maximilian said; then they stood by the tan Volkswagen. They bought coffee, hot chocolate for Vee and they sat on a bench put there for just sitting on. Vee stumbled across green mowed grass, Winn bought vended potato chips, a Mars bar. They'd have to keep their dog leashed if they had a dog, but they could have planned a crime, smoked some crack. He walked a diaper daintily to the can where you weren't supposed to do that on the sign.

Then they talked about France: she would have preferred it, he guessed; then she showed him Billy Neal's grandmothers' rings that she'd also stolen.

There's always a little story, a small mystery left.

We could always have done anything that we wanted, she said.

Those grandmothers' rings were wedding rings.

There's even a Camden Drive, Camden Yards, we could watch the Orioles lose there, he said. The Shot Tower, famous places.

You'll probably marry me there, Winn said.

He'd have stopped the car if they hadn't been already stopped to get gas. He'd have got out and knelt in the snow, if there had been snow, but it was still fall so he knelt on the asphalt between the 8 and 9 pump.

Would you? he said.

You mean *me*? Her smile had no sarcasm.

She walked away from the pumps, walking her thoughts like carrying water along a rough road in a too-shallow pan. He was almost sixty, he'd never been wed, she was nearly forty and she'd been, just once, but a very long time, if this meant anything. She was still wearing the white escape dress which seemed, now, appropriate.

She came back.

He said, this is a lot to happen, I guess.

She looked down at him, she held Vee. Do you think it's good luck to get married with Billy Neal's rings?

Luck, Vee said like she knew what it meant. Yes, Winn said, I say yes.

Rain leaked in the windwing, he sang that old song about counting the cars on the New Jersey Turnpike though they weren't there yet. Winn slept with her shoulder on his while he drove with one hand and it wasn't easy but he put a ring on her finger, the other on his.

I'm awake, Max, Winn said. That was the most romantic thing. She was laughing at him.

Daylight, the truckers looked down, the pigs in their fat SUVs, cowboys in the Greyhound. She'd painted her toenails and nails, and Vee's, her hair clipped back from her forehead. His hands on the wheel, her hand on his wrist. Her ring. His. Anyone could see it.

He thought Baltimore would be like stepping into a memory, but no, he told Winn. They stood by the Belvedere Arms with the pink diaper bag and brown sack with her underwear and his, her spare blouse, he'd forgot his toothbrush. You're sad you're not sadder, Winn said.

Sad would have been fine. He wanted the way he'd been, here, before: that old could-be-happiness.

He carried Vee up all hundreds of Shot Tower steps and tried looking out backwards through time. The city had got fixed up, some. A tiny Potemkin downtown, like new laces threading old shoes, but he already had the reels from this place in his head.

From their kitchen window you saw sky, trees with trembly leaves. Clothes in the window; it rained, rainwater beaded the glass, Winn tested the bed, the Bolex was still under it.

Why don't you use it, she said.

He thought he felt he believed he imagined he wondered (even). . . . Baltimore got in the way of itself, is what he could have said.

Yeah yeah, Winn would say, like talking's the same as doing something about it.

An effort was necessary so he emptied his pockets from change and Winn opened her uniform buttons in front while Vee slept, like this was something they could do about it, or instead.

He rolled down the stockings she wore for the long windy walk to the cold-tiled dinette where she served sandwiches. Her watch ticked in his hair and he took her wrist to see how much time they had left.

You're not paying attention, Winn said.

Baltimore made him clumsy, its places and thoughts that weren't even there anymore yet he stumbled on them.

Outside: kind of bleak, kind of grey, kind of windswept.

For all the pictures about Winn, she wasn't them. *Moving* pictures, sure, but they were just pictures that moved.

After the sobering house he used to come out of a movie and drive around on the lighted nighttime rainy streets and he felt like the whole world came in and the world went out of him to meet it.

To him, Winn was like this. Not, the-body-the-brain.

Once he'd tried to tell her, in Camden, but she did the thing with her wrist, the thing with her hair. She'd said okay okay Max.

He'd felt it when they wore themselves out in bed. Tall, walking away from behind, her pale unabashed behind.

You looking at my happy ass?

She was going to put water on for Instant. Get a paper towel for their mess. Snail tracks he scraped with his nails—sometimes he didn't wash her off. Drove around like that. He did ordinary things that were made extraordinary from it.

The movie was meant to explain this but of course it couldn't.

She'd said, yeah, no reason to make it, then. Her voice put in the exclamation.

Her bare heels on the floor like when Werner thumped the mute and the echo pedals. Ink from his fingerprints where he rubbed his fingers on the score.

I always felt sorry for you, Werner said at the airport motel, which meant he felt sorry for himself. That's what he composed: pity for all mankind, which meant, really, no pity for anyone. Kind of like Winn but different; mercy's not the same thing, is it?

Winn came back to bed, her age showed on her elbows; that's where it shows first.

Seen enough? she said. Just enough to be sentimental about, I bet.

Like driving around on some slick glossy street after the movie ended.

The snapshot camera dangled from his wrist, it cost ninety-nine cents, he might trick himself yet into making the movie again. He was searching through time for the past he kept bringing to it, even though he was making it up; still, no less real for that.

The camera leaked light on the hopeful apartments on narrower streets. Police horses steamed, hooves stamping the snow, their white breaths though it hadn't snowed yet. The harbor and Fort Holabird. He looked for himself but he wasn't that guy.

He held Vee's hand under his—here, push the shutter, kid—he showed her how to make accidents: his ankles, hers, some quick bird sky left behind—he couldn't have done any better himself. Vee didn't get how you saw the picture you got and maybe she was right.

Afternoon turned to late afternoon and the room was too small. His mind was too small. Winn lay on the bed with rain from the open window on her legs. She tilted her knees toward his. A picture? she said.

Winn cut out beneath Darwin's sky, reflected on Harleigh Lake with her hair and the water windswept, Winn against Texas's barrenness.

She smiled, damp teeth white. He felt nostalgic for her even now, giddy with irresoluteness.

You're scared you'll be finished she said though he wasn't but he didn't know what he was and how do you take any pictures of that?

Winn touched his leg by the bed. You're too stubborn she said, though you don't even know what about.

He took the film to a one-hour place although what was the rush? Birds flew through milk. Baltimore all fogged up. You do what you can with whatever you get: pictures of what wasn't there anymore, and Winn's knees, after all.

It seemed foreordained like the dream where you're kissing the beautiful stranger but he didn't always read people right: tragic or tragic acting? He thought the girl planned her leaning against him that made him go all-right-all-right with his hand on her dark wavy hair though she seemed obviously, naively, maybe calculating. Some sweet powdery scent like an overstatement.

He hadn't smelled perfume on a girl since—never. The old man's girlfriends.

They sat in the long sideways seats on the M23 toward North Bend: you could see yourself in the glass and just headlights and signs and stores lit inside. Everyone dreamy and tired, it must have been from dreaminess why they kissed and who anyway started it? Maybe he could split the difference. Perhaps it was not on purpose; maybe it was a real accident.

She tasted like he had forgot what a new person's kissing is like. Her mouth was cool, the bus cold but her skin wasn't cold. Winn and Vee had the cold, he'd rubbed Vaporub on their chest and his hands still smelled like it.

He had no papers that said he couldn't. That's why there are laws of marriage: the paper's what makes it happen.

Her little phone chirped in her jeans and she looked and twisted her mouth and snapped it (the phone) shut. Everybody has something going on.

Outside, the rain would hold off, the light in the bus foreclosed disguises. Chipped paint on her quick-bitten nails, her Mediterranean hair, an Italian girl with her own mafia of affections and plans.

Francine don't call me Fran.

He smiled ruefully wistfully ironically when she got up to get off past his stop so he'd have to ride back. She was a moving picture in the glass or the picture behind her moved fast.

Make another like '79. He could have cut old pieces in, hoped for irony but that's no kind of hope to wish for. A fool when you put a camera in his hand. That's why he'd kissed Francine. He carried it like a secret surprise he kept springing on his own mind.

Sometimes he thought he only imagined Winn figured it out.

She wrung her uniform over the tub, he spooned Gerbers into Vee's mouth. Their happy tent now was the sheet on their knees and for hide and seek with Vee. He hid there, too, away from Winn's eyes, in her duskier feminine wiles. If he even tried not to try some technique . . .

When wouldn't she tell him she guessed? He was careful down there. He was too old and smart to confess. The narrow window filtered the afternoon light of justice.

Safer on the bus. Afternoon clouds clumped like mattress batting, you could smell rain in them. He watched power lines rise and dip like when he was a kid, the swoopy rides behind Werner's not-dressed-in-white brides, beside the orchestra instruments.

Baltimore the old sore, the old scores.

The square blocks, the sidewalks, Fran's building the white of a dirty Styrofoam cup. His snapshot camera leaked a milky fog all over his unexposed film. He'd have wound it to the next frame but it got stuck between desire and fact and he wouldn't film that. Anyway, he already had.

He'd take one picture, quick, if it rained, then he stood in the rain in shirtsleeves. When he drank he'd made deals with himself. He put his hands in his pockets and went whistling warily down the street. His yellow plastic camera dangling.

In 1979 he could still go to a bar. You could drive around and take pictures of any buildings and you got away with things.

In every instance the whole past repeats itself until you catch up to now. The trick would be to stop your brain there: a weather like you rolled your own cigarettes with chapped hands, you pulled your sleeves over your palms.

Winn put on a dress like she'd looked back then. Do you like this blue skirt?

She hadn't had a real autumn with him. A winter with snow. Well, Camden but that was an emergency. Those dying leaves too sad when they changed and fell. She'd forgot this is how Baltimore might be for Max.

Had he gone to see that dead girl from before? Winn didn't want to say the girl's name, she remembered he'd invented it.

Almost raining now. Winn could have waltzed around in her underpants, the radiator steamed everything up. He liked a room where you had to keep all your clothes on and sleeping like that. It focused the mind. But for what?

I still miss the desert, Winn said. His room and her room. Dick Legg always going away or the big welcome back. She sat beside Max on the bed. Unhappiness comes from the search to be happy he'd said but now he never talked when he should.

She wanted to put on a coat and have a cocktail in it with her purse beside her on the bar, maybe even smoke with her elbows up. She saw it clear as a picture he could have taken: wherever there's a need there's a lack.

Her uniform under her wool navy coat, the cigarette odd in her hand. Can you live like this, without unhappiness? She felt attended. She felt a guy's smile. It's true that smoke gets in your eyes.

He struggled putting the bright yellow raincoat on Vee so laughing is how Francine caught him; that would stick. She looked at Vee. She gave him an unhappy smile.

Yeah my kid. He didn't have to say it.

Coffee? Or something? he said.

She kept flashing the smile off and on. Oh sure coffee, Francine said. Look, walk me to work.

He usually never talked because look how it went.

Clerk clerk clerk, Francine said, that's my dumb cluck job.

He held Vee's hand and Francine walked alongside his other side not touching as they went. Wind blew her hair into his and he was trying to see her face and hold Vee and Vee's toy and the diaper bag.

Francine said, we sell stuff to carwash stores. You know. License plate frames with your name. Those smell things like Christmas trees.

He put Vee on his other hip. What did it matter what's said, it doesn't make whatever happens.

She walked fast. I don't guess you smoke, hardly

nobody smokes. Francine laughed. Why am I even asking, she said, I have some. She pulled out a Kool.

For you I'd start, he said.

Ha! she said.

Vee wanted to get down and up and he put her down and picked her up. Francine looked at Vee and he didn't say, yeah and we kissed. I'm not a big talker, he said, unless you want to talk about Marx.

She crushed out her cigarette. Okay what about Marx.

I don't know. He laughed. He had nothing to say about Marx, about movies, even, he couldn't talk smartly about anything though he knew what he liked.

We looked at the big boats, he said. "Big boats." Winn laughed. She put out the setups, she wiped down the table, she wiped at Vee's mouth with the rag. Jesus, I didn't do that.

He showed her the toy he got Vee, the Goofy you pressed on its base to make dance.

She said, you're the dog.

You, he said. Bite worse than bark.

The Bolex stayed under the bed.

Who's Francine? Whose Francine would he be looking at? If the past is made up from right now, then the now is the future, he thought, so whatever happens has already happened, ahead.

Francine tapped her cigarette on its pack. He had the snapshot camera out, he saw how she might get used to this.

Wind blew dirt through the bus stop. Across the street people came out from the jail and stood smoking, cold, on the sidewalk. Sometimes a furtive car picked someone up. Francine let out her white breath. Are we just going to keep doing this?

Sure, the bus benches of Baltimore tour, Maximilian said.

But it was after '79 he was thinking about. Well what did he think about it? An orange-brown quilt on the bed, a dresser, a TV he kept mostly turned off. Cold like this. Like he'd got locked out of a house and two dozen years passed.

Clouds blew in from the lake like large wedding cakes; he was still that guy and he hadn't married Winn yet.

He had Vee's toy in his coat, really he'd got it for Winn and himself. Look, Francine. He made Goofy dance. Let's go look at the big boats, he said.

These snapshots: Francine's busman's tour around Baltimore, Winn's oilcloth tablecloth. She tossed the pictures on the bed. You'd take mine if I was more naked I bet, she said.

They were meant to be practice for making the movie but Winn wouldn't film. If he left the Bolex under the bed he couldn't betray Winn with it is how his thinking went.

The kitchen with light reflected from snow or the sky. This isn't how we wanted to live, Maximilian said.

Crazy police cars raced by in the street, gunplay in the stairwells.

Well. Winn laughed.

Our bourgeois rhapsody, or is it the threepenny operetta, he said.

Winn pinched some salt into the Kraft. She ate any kind of crap. He loved that. She smelled nice. Her mouth used to taste like the desert. *Oh man.* His eyes welled. Oh good Christ. He looked out at the weepy clouds. He despaired in his grey underwear in grey afternoon light. Could he make himself feel any worse. He would try.

She poured the warm Kool Aid with extra sugar for the kid. She said, please stop suffering, Max.

He'd been reading about the eternal return. It meant you should act like if you had to do it again you would do the same thing, he told Winn.

Winn stacked her tips on the bed, the coins tipped. Like forget to get married, she said.

The heater an anvil accompaniment to Winn singing here comes the bride but she's laughing at him, how he lived on her kindness and she simply lived.

Vee had the snapshots in her mouth. At opposite corners they held out their arms, come on Vee, Viv, Evelyn, then he crossed the floor so he'd stand by Winn's side. Ah, let's don't make the kid choose, he said.

She should remember this: windy, cold; she wore white. Max so handsome in his Goodwill suit, Vee in her little Goodwill dress. But Winn blew the rent on hers, maybe he'd film her in it though he didn't bring even the snapshot camera along. He wasn't taking pictures of Winn anymore. She'd thought art and life were the same for him because hadn't it been?

Her dress looked whiter than any snow that might have fallen all over North Gay and she'd sprung for a cab and how should she feel about riding around in a cab?

Cold but she wouldn't ruin the dress by wearing a sweater or coat though she couldn't feel her arms anymore, her hand with the winter flowers.

Funny: just a taxi. Black trees. Dudes prancing around the puddles protecting their high-toned shoes.

They'd took off their rings so they could put them back as groom and bride. She'd had her hair set in wild curls, so clean in her dress is how come she knew what she'd smelled on Max was cigarette smoke or did she bring it back from the bar. So would it be good or bad if Max had holes in his Goodwill pockets where a ring could fall out. Still, she held her peace, they placed their bets with the hopeful, nervous.

After, they walked hands in Vee's hands, rehearsing *my husband my wife* alongside the love-me-or-not Eager Street railroad ties, with Vee the circuit between them.

A little tired, a little compromised, a little surprised they're not more surprised. Winn a cloudy day feast for sore eyes with her loopy hair and how they're suddenly diffident: Winn a bit blue in white, Max's dark suit's blued pants, Vee's shiny face in the bright overcast. Soon they'd lie down if Vee allowed it. Would it be different tonight? A little anxious, like newlyweds.

Could you make a movie about Baltimore that didn't put Baltimore in it? A Baltimore of the mind. Well what isn't of that? But he did like Francine and she should have been the film now.

Sure and Winn smiled from the bed in her coat, Vee's sleep-damped hair under her hands. She knew there was something that happened with Max that was still going on.

He'd wait for the rain. Meanwhile, he practiced: "Francine, everything counts. Francine I said my vows."

Well, the bus went where she lived. Francine smiled sweetly—what he took sweetly to be, so he didn't say any of it. She sat on her steps, her fingertips stained with GPS filters, whatever; nervous-kneed—something spiky about Francine and how her shoulders dipped. A weight on the small girl. She talked fast to shake it.

He could have filmed her in Frank Boceck Park in front of the statue of Corporal someone. Her sick dad in the Apt apartments in the radiation of the television.

Her pencil-thin legs, the soaked rabbityness of Francine. She looked like a social welfare argument. Like by her loudness she'd prove that she hadn't been run to the ground, judged. She was what Marxism was about and how Marxism lied.

They walked under the street where the storm drain went under the park and came up from the tunnel of unmarried love. Francine flicked her cigarette butt. You're one of those *girl-saving* guys aren't you Max.

Well sure, used to be, but not *now*.

But what beneficence he'd once had! He'd bring hope like soft cloned sheepish clouds, he'd be the cool rain on a young girl's bare feet on a burning sidewalk if there was a sidewalk. Then, wind would whip bright thankful tears from her tight narrow smile. Ah, Francine, I thought the full moon would rise over us like the fiery bust of Karl Marx.

Wasn't that, still, what his film was about? But he'd never make that movie twice—even once.

She'd forgot to take off her paper tiara or punch the time clock. Why shouldn't she know what she didn't know that she already guessed? Winn closed her eyes, poked her umbrella along the sidewalk. Navigating by luck.

The girl skinny enough Winn could see the head of Karl Marx on the book she sat on on the steps. A good picture for Max. Winn's brain said to use the part of her brain that should pay attention.

Too, the girl wore Maximilian's coat; how many greatcoats like that could there be in Baltimore? And Max was a Communist now, he was sharing the wealth.

But Winn didn't gloat though she felt the joy of evidence. She sat beside Francine's shiny knees, the girl's shoes thin enough they might as well have been paper shoes.

Max up there?

The girl lit a quick cigarette in a delinquent way Winn understood. Winn waited for Francine to say it's a free country for sitting on steps. *She* would have. She saw herself take off her dress in the heat of big open spaces. She could have been judged. In some circumstances.

So should I go away now? Francine said.

Winn laughed. Should we have you over for Christmas?

The girl shrugged. Your kid likes me, she said.

Winn stood. The clouds had that tarnished silver before rain, then it rained. Any cab could have taken her anyplace along Gay but no! And sit in some black and white film like Max's? Well, not like his. What was she going to do, make a Bergman movie out of this?

Francine cupped her hand like some Bowery Boy to her next cigarette. The rain wouldn't hurt anyone but Winn opened her new umbrella and held it over them: only a fool would insist on the romance of rain on your head.

Francine had smoked two cigarettes, kept the Marx. She staggered a little in the unsteady distance.

Winn shivered: Baltimore: she suddenly didn't like it.

When you go see her, she said, what do you guys talk about?

Maximilian thought Francine had miscalculated but he wouldn't betray that one kiss. Quantity made the quality of it. He needed her for this movie that seemed to have started without him holding the camera on it.

Darwin, I told her about Darwin, he said.

I bet you want to go there, Winn said. Start again. This time we'll tell about ourselves.

She was just talking, he thought. It would never happen. You know everything about me but not vice versa, he said.

Not all your girlfriends' names though, Winn said. Somehow it now seemed important.

He said, I wrote them down once, I kept it in a German book, and the names of all the cars. The little

Toyota that couldn't. The van that didn't clear the clearance.

They laughed, they looked at each other to see that they'd laughed. Maximilian said you can't leave me until Vee's eighteen at least.

Winn said, will you sleep with Francine?

Well, I don't *have* to, he said.

Don't think I'd ever be happy about it, Winn said.

Me neither he said like now happiness could be removed from them.

I didn't sleep with as many people as you think, Winn said.

I never thought that.

Not with you at first for a long time, she said, as if he might have forgotten that.

How they'd watched one another asleep in the car, head bumping against the window or tipped back open-mouthed.

He took Winn's hand, they stood like that for a while until they really did have to go up.

He said, It's gonna be fine.

Cold wind blew on them. Okay, she said. Don't say it.

Go make your movie but make it quickly Winn said.

He carried the Bolex wrapped in plastic from the rain. He'd looked at so many things to make pictures from, he didn't like noticing, anymore, anything.

Well too late; he'd spent thirty years doing it.

There was a Westinghouse clock and birds outside calling the dusk. Francine sat up against where the headboard should be and smoked. Traffic went by, she hadn't turned on a light but then he turned on all the lights. She looked skinny and pale like if you saw her through X-ray specs. She looked *sinny* he thought, but he didn't dare be imaginative.

Francine packed a bong. Bubble clouds clouded the room.

Don't even offer me some, I'm paranoid enough, Maximilian said.

His Marx and her mittens dried on the heater, she'd been carrying it everywhere. Francine had marks-a-lotted Marx's face. Black eyes. Devil's horns. The heater hissed and moaned, clanged an anvil chorus. Well Marx too if you thought about it.

Contact high. Maximilian laughed.

Francine laughed too—who knew what a young girl thought? If you don't use that camera then what's the purpose? she said.

Like Marx without revolution, he said.

Like here you are but no kissing she said. She lay across her childhood bed and made a snow angel on the sheet. She said her new year's resolve was to grow hair under her arms and not shave her legs. For Darwin, she said.

Outside, a Bing Crosby snow melted over a burning trashcan. Winn would have gone down with Vee and tasted Baltimore in the flakes.

It's hot there I bet, Francine said.

Actually it would be really cold now but he wouldn't spoil Francine's version. He felt hopeful and cheered. The snow and the banging racket and burning smelly gloves, that dream like a pipeful carried them.

The street's soft-duned snows in the morning before the snowplows. No difference between the sidewalk and the street except the parked cars' round white mounds; benevolent blurry streetlights and Christmas lights.

He high-stepped with his Bolex on before the plows dirtied everything up.

He also had pictures of sky and lights on the water like blurred time-lapsed stars.

It was a secret he kept from even himself, how he'd exposed Baltimore for weeks now, sunlight if there was some, or that dangerous sailors' dawn pinked like Winn's arms when she stayed in the sun: his movie about only light—well all movies are. A movie about before thoughts, then God had His thought.

He turned off the Bolex, people were coming out now. Sometimes he sat for an hour with the camera on his lap: there is no naked eye.

Okay but he'd taken pictures around Camden Yards and the Naval something for Winn.

Are these an apology or an accusation? she'd said.

Dark came at five and they looked at cocktail signs and he bought Winn a drink and Vee ate the peanuts. Everybody wore coats in the bar, he liked that, ladies and men in their coats and hats at bars where men kept their hats on. He bequeathed it the irony of his smile: his nostalgia like how you remember the parts of a movie that weren't even in it but that's what it's really about.

Is this okay? To come in here? Winn said.

He felt glad she remembered she knew something about him.

They held hands, Vee between them, but still, Winn a little unsteady outside. No darker at nine than before, not like when he drank years went by. A little regret. The streetlights polished it.

Snow and rain, you could trust it. You couldn't hold the weather against anyone. No sky in the car, the Xmas lights winked white and blue tiny hopes and he had hopeful thoughts that you wouldn't call thinking at all.

Francine could talk all night long in the Datsun she suddenly had but she wasn't talking now. He could have even slept, his head rattling against the cold glass, though she made it hard: her arrangement with skids, arguments with stoplights. He watched dark go past, then picture windows, everything you could buy whipped away into night.

The moon cold, his loaded camera on the seat, the rain stopped. Can a thought cross across a small car?

My dad's dead, Francine said in the fishy moonlight. She'd painted her fingernails blue but she bit them so all you could see was the bits of blue left.

Oh Fran, Maximilian said.

She touched the dumb hat she'd put on his head— it was not lost on him—which was her father's hat. She held the beer can in her knees like he used to hold whiskey there; she said, you still can't call me that.

He thought about Werner unredeemed, unassailable now in that future from where memories come. He thought about Winn, how whenever they'd been two alone they'd soon enough added a third; then there could be two together, and the other one.

He said, so Francine, now what?

Francine chewed gum and smoked and waved her driving hands around. Why drink beer it just makes me cold makes me pee, Francine said as she parked and they walked up the Belvedere's steps and he filmed the dark stairs from behind.

Marx said it's not theory but action that counts, but he'd stopped reading Marx.

Just make some pictures, Max.

The snow kept stopping. The girls kept talking. He couldn't go see Francine now; Francine was upstairs. They were powdering their breasts, bouncing Vee on their knees, not talking about him.

He held the Bolex on his knee on the steps. *Don't even bring it up to your eye.* A trash truck smashed by, the snowplow. The bright winter sun. He thought about Baltimore from before, how he'd been hopeless, and yet . . .

Winn came downstairs to check up on him, Francine came down. Winn's shift. Francine's shift. They stepped down the stairs with their coats blowing open and mittens and gave him the eyes of worry. They gave each other the eye about him.

You can't stand this, Winn said. She knew what it meant when he slept in his clothes and that he hadn't slept.

He nodded. The tag-team, he said.

Francine lit a smoke and she passed it to Winn. One day we'll stand here and where's Max? Francine said.

Going backwards and getting ahead of myself, Maximilian said. The morning snow already stained by daylight, what was *now* was a future he'd never arrive at, he thought.

The smoke blew away from Winn's mouth. You're not happy here are you, she said.

Well, he said, unhappiness.

Winn passed him the cigarette. The wet snow in the street made the cars sound like mush. You can go if you want, we'll still be us, she said.

The wind stopped and he smoked although he didn't smoke and he squinted at Winn. When the wind stops, he said, the smoke now in his eyes, is it still, then, the wind?

The rain that would turn into snow came down hard on Francine's little car. *Drums Along the Mohawk.* They'd be scalping the settlers in the next reel but he'd run out of what happens next. He had just his little enthusiasms—the film stock he liked, soft cotton tee-shirts with V-necks.

Baltimore looked like winter in Baltimore while he got in the car, Francine nervous-kneed trailing cigarette smoke on the steps. Winn smoked, too: Winn and the picture of Winn. It occurred to him, the future of what happened with the Bolex between them had caught up to them.

He had the camera on the seat. He saw his breath, like a screen, and he wiped the windshield. Winn tapped the glass, *roll it down,* and he thought about taking off Winn's nylons and everything.

Francine held Vee up: the bribe. *No way, man.*

He touched his own movie guy's face where the camera had blindsided him. He looked along Gay like someone who didn't take pictures of things. Parked cars, a few trees. Some people had left their wash out, it had frozen and thawed but he didn't want to make anything out of it.

There stood love on the sidewalk while poor people passed, looking dangerous. He looked at his wife and kid and girlfriend. He thought about taking a picture but he knew what they looked like. Everyone knew what everything was and that was the problem.

He'd drive to the sea and throw the Bolex overboard. He'd got what he wanted to get and he had now only to lose it.

The Chesapeake emptied into the fog. Where were the sailors? They'd gone off to war. Well that's what they were sailors for.

He looked in the ashtray for a butt. He looked in his brain at his film. This seascape. He wouldn't film it.

Oh, he was stubborn, even Winn said.

He could picture her with the phone pushed to her ear against the traffic on Gay. Fog on the phone booth's glass. Other pictures from Baltimore he hadn't taken.

You can go if you want, Winn said.

He stood by the weeds by the technically stolen Datsun, though he hadn't crossed a state line. He liked these small no man's lands, these tiny forests.

What we have, Winn said, it's not about geography, Max.

The keys on the counter, all he'd had to do was lift them. He said, I'm still in Maryland, Winn.

She laughed, so he didn't say he'd already got gas, he'd ate a whole package of little chocolate donuts.

Look at the moon, it's the same moon, Winn said, though there was no moon where he stood, only the weeds he'd just filmed. What he had so far: the weeds, no moonlight; from behind, Francine's ass going up the dark steps.

Winn breathed in the phone. I'm not saying anything to Vee, she said and he felt proud abashed she was fighting for them.

They listened a while to the electric sea on the line.

You like it this way, the ether between us, Winn said.

He nodded though she couldn't see. Yeah not too close. He laughed.

His voice was right there, as close as he got and she kind of liked how that was.

He looked at the cars going by; if he cradled the phone he could even film them while talking to Winn.

She heard the distance and the clicking Bolex. She rubbed the phone booth's fogged glass, tapped her ring like good luck but he didn't see that. The snow fell, but that's all it was, some weather between them.

My daddy, mister macaroni and cheese, Francine said. The blanket in his lap. His ashes on the dashboard and she'd been more places already than he ever went, Francine said.

Winn dried Francine's hair with the towel, patted blush on her zitty forehead.

But here we are bundled up safe from the wind and the snow and the *ghetto*, Francine said. She shook out her new wet red nails. Poor daddy, she said, not even getting to step in puddles anymore. No one to play checkers with. Scared to die in his awful blanket, and then when he knew that's just what would happen.

While she closed her door and blew pot. While she kept edging the car toward the edges of Maryland.

He'd like to see Darwin I bet, Francine said. The sand dunes, the camels, the Nile flowing muddily past the Sphinx. I'm saving his ashes for scattering there.

Don't count on it, Winn said. She had the big curlers out. You want TV hair, we'll use these, see? Big as soup cans, Fran, she said.

Okay you can call me that, Francine said. Her underwear dried on the radiator next to Winn's while Winn wound her hair on the rollers and stepped back and laughed.

Francine said, aren't you mad about me and Max? Like you're okay with that?

Winn pushed the pack of Newports toward Fran. Don't set yourself on fire. Go ahead, smoke us out.

I'll teach you to, too, Francine said.

It's not like I haven't before, Winn said.

Sure, you've done everything, Francine said.

Winn lit a cigarette, put it between Francine's lips, took one out for herself. Well, you will, too, she said. She'd fixed her up nicely for when Max came back. You've already started, she said.

Vee was up, she was up. Still dark, they were eating Cheerios from the box. No Daddy, Vee said. It was conversation enough.

Winn sweeping Cheerios at dawn. Just last week he'd showed her some of the film. She hadn't guessed about so many times she'd been watched. All the places he said don't wave but she had, the parts where she turned from the lens.

She stood in the phone booth and smoked all the Newports Francine left.

I miss you but I like missing you, too, he said. The whole idea was I have nothing to say, and here I am, saying, he said.

He could hear Winn smoking. The delay in the line. It's like when the mind thinks it's thinking, who's thinking? he said.

Winn rolled her eyes but he couldn't see that. She said, nothing's like anything, Max.

You don't even expect me to come back, he said.

He slept in the car. He drove around the greenery and asphalt of outer Maryland. The clouds were low or high, the trees tall then small. Water stood or froze or had frozen in tire-gouged mud. Winn in his head and everywhere rags like small flags in the bushes in wind or no wind. He stopped and peed and bought coffee and had to pee again. Trying to get lost on the small roads, to wander away by accident.

He parked and ran his hands through his dirty hair like some answer might get scratched up there.

The idea of talking. Change for the phone. He bought a pack of Pall Malls with the notion of smoking along while they talked.

The cloud cover lay low over the next area code, he could go and be there with himself, anywhere, but how close could he get?

She'd taken a bus and hitchhiked. She'd come all the way to Bethesda, he'd called her, he wanted to ask her how Winn really was.

And me of course, Francine said. How I am.

Of course, too, he could have just asked on the phone but he'd waited outside the Greyhound, then she'd jumped from a van like Winn had, almost.

What do you think you're doing, Francine said, which Winn wouldn't have asked.

Thinking and doing, that's two different things, Maximilian said.

They walked by ships and sailors and the romantic sea with whitecaps. We could all go to Darwin, she said. Or just you and me can.

He just wanted to look at her sneakers, white socks, without thinking he wanted them in his film. That's not in the choices, he said.

Francine shrugged. Too much guilt I suppose.

He could have asked if Winn knew she had come but that shouldn't make a difference. Meanwhile, crisp sunlight, Francine happy to find him, him glad to be found. Hand in hand almost like pals, who had kissed.

The happy daylight, then cold sullen dusk, which could have been fine except they'd have to stop walking and talk. Not that we *have* to she said though she knew what he meant.

We'll sleep in the Datsun, he said.

Or not sleep, she said.

Or you could go back.

Ah, she said; she'd borrowed the inflection from Winn. You want to keep your freedom, I guess.

Not that it could be lost except as a thought. Through an act. And then the afterthought.

She promised herself, no more candles, but here they were, flickering.

He'll be back, Francine said.

At six Max would call, say out loud some of what he'd rehearsed all night long. While Winn stood in the telephone booth, shivering. Tweakers tapping on the glass. *Hurry up fucken bitch.*

I'm joining a band, Francine said, we're going to Buffalo, dude.

Winn pictured Francine with dreads, torn skateboard-kneed pants. Experiences, who shouldn't have them, Winn said.

Francine packed her tee-shirt, underpants. I wouldn't want to be you though when I get your age, Francine said.

Winn looked up; Francine was kind of smiling. So gimme a souvenir, Francine said.

The film lay around; Winn had watched Max enough, it's not like she didn't know how, so, okay, she cut into it.

A piece of Darwin. Some parts of her several hairstyles.

Francine put the strips in her bag. She paced like Max, held the bag to her chest, practicing how you left.

I went to meet him, you know, Francine said.

Sure you did, Winn said.

Francine frowned. Her shadow grew long and shrank. Maybe nothing happened, she said.

Maybe. Winn laughed. It was loud in the small apartment.

I'm gonna play drums, Francine said.

Winn woke Vee. Here, kiss Frannie goodbye.

Drums or guitar, Francine said to herself. Do I even know how?

Winn carried Vee to the window, looked out. It's just banging and strumming, you fake it and all of a sudden you're playing for real, kid, she said.

He propped the Bolex on the ledge of one of the last two real telephone booths in the U.S. There's a bunch of stupid things I could do now, he said. I may not do any of them.

Except the thing you're doing now, though, Winn said, though she said it with some laughing in it.

I'm making the plan for the good fruitful years ahead, Winn. He looked at the camera and shrugged, he wanted to make silly faces. Remind me what you always say, Winn, he said.

Like, never explain?

And nothing is unconditional, he said.

Except what we have and not even that, Max, Winn said.

Outside the booth, it would rain, it already started. How's Vee? How's Francine? he said. Never mind, they're just fine.

Winn laughed.

I'm making the movie right now, because that's my job, I guess, he said. He held the unlit cigarette. This soul-searching stuff! Man! he said.

There's no soul, there's just what you do, Max, Winn said.

Rain would sweep across him on the way to the car but he wouldn't mind even if the Bolex got wet. It's going to rain hard, he said.

You probably want to stay out of it, Max, but you probably won't. Am I right?

He nodded but she couldn't see that, the rain streaking the glass, the Datsun. You've always been the best philosopher, Winn. And wife mother lover, he said. He lit his Pall Mall. Really coming down now. He heard Winn lighting hers.

Hang in there, Max, soon you'll be rolling the credits, she said.

The match, the inhale, the blue smoke: first he'd have to put this part in.

THE END

L‍ES P‍LESKO was born in Budapest and was educated at UCLA. He is the author of the novel, *The Last Bongo Sunset*, which was translated into Dutch and German, and his stories have appeared in *Zyzzyva* and *Pear Noir!*. To date he has been a cotton shoveler, pool cleaner, gas station attendant, furniture refinisher, grape-picker, crop-duster's flagman, ditch digger, farmhand, modeling school and cemetary plot salesperson, Catholic-school English teacher, boiler-room solicitor, dispatcher, trade show consultant, country-and-western disc jockey, and freelance writer. He is editor of the medical journal *Neonatal Intensive Care* and instructor in the UCLA Writers Program and lives in Venice, California.

SLOW LIE
DETECTOR
SET IN
ADOBE GARAMOND

LAYOUT DESIGN
NORMAN TUTTLE
ALPHA DESIGN & COMPOSITION

PRINTED BY
HIGNELL BOOK PRINTING

PHOTOGRAPHY
MAX CHOW

COVER DESIGN
MICHAEL DEYERMOND

PUBLISHED BY
EQUATOR BOOKS PUBLISHING
VENICE, CA